It had rained every day for a week in Smurf Village and the awful weather was making everyone feel sad and gloomy.

Hmm. Everyone complains about the weather, but no one ever does anything to smurf it, thought Handy Smurf one morning. Suddenly, he had a brainstorm and hurried over to draw up his plans.

After many hours, Handy's idea began to take shape. He had created a machine that ran on floodwater.

Handy invited all the Smurfs to see his invention. They huddled together in the pouring rain.

"Now watch closely," Handy said. "I just smurf this lever, and a door will open in the roof. A wooden Smurf wearing a bathing suit will appear!"

Immediately, the clouds disappeared, and bright sunlight filled the sky. All the Smurfs jumped for joy and shouted, "Hooray!"

But when Handy pushed the lever back, a wooden Smurf carrying a mushroom umbrella appeared. Instantly the rain returned!

Handy pushed another lever that released a strong wind.
"Handy, your invention is smurf-tastic," yelled Papa Smurf. "But please, smurf back the nice weather!"

To celebrate the beautiful weather, the Smurfs decided to have a big picnic. Poet Smurf was so inspired he began writing a new poem, "An Ode to the Sun."

Everyone was having a great time and enjoying the sunshine. Everyone that is, except Farmer Smurf. He was unhappy because his vegetables were wilting!

"What my vegetables need is a nice, smurfy little shower," he said. So he set off to find Handy's weather machine.

Suddenly the beautiful weather disappeared and rain poured down even harder than before.

"Oh no! I need good weather to finish my poem," Poet Smurf said.
And he set off to find Handy's weather machine too.
Poet Smurf had just brought the sunshine back
when Farmer Smurf appeared, demanding the rain.

"Rain for my lettuce!" Farmer Smurf shouted.

"Sunshine for my poem!" Poet Smurf yelled back.

The two argued while pushing and pulling on the levers of the weather machine.

BOOM! Suddenly the weather began changing from one second to the next! Rain turned into sunshine and then into a blizzard!

Hmm. Something isn't smurfing quite right with my machine, Handy thought. *I'd better go and check it out.*

Meanwhile, Poet Smurf and Farmer Smurf were still fighting. But the fight ended when thick black smoke began to pour out of the weather machine.

"We're not going to be able to smurf this by ourselves," said Farmer Smurf. "We need to go and find Handy Smurf!"

On their way, they met Handy, who was heading towards the weather machine. "What's going on?" he asked.

"We used your machine. I'm sorry. I think it's a little bit smurfed," Poet Smurf said sadly.

"Oh no!" Handy exclaimed. "We have to stop this before it smurfs a catastrophe! Let's go and find Papa and fix the weather machine!"

Handy, Farmer Smurf, and Poet Smurf found Papa and some others and hurried back to the weather machine. But on their way, a very strong wind blew a huge tree trunk into the river. Just as they were about to cross a bridge, the tree smashed into it, and the bridge broke into pieces.

"Hurry!" yelled Papa Smurf. "We're going to have to smurf a big detour to reach the weather machine."

Just then, it got very foggy. The Smurfs couldn't see their noses in front of their faces!

The weather continued to change as the Smurfs made their way to the machine. One minute it was raining, the next it was snowing, and the next there was a thunderstorm!

When the Smurfs finally reached the weather machine, they were caught in a hurricane that swirled and blew them around like bits of straw.

Handy was able to reach the levers but he could not stop the machine. Then he smurfed an idea. He asked Brainy for his umbrella, made it into a kite, and tied the string to the weather machine.

All of a sudden, lightning hit the kite, travelled through the long string, and smashed the weather machine to pieces!

It wasn't long before the weather calmed down and everything returned to normal.

"I'm sorry about your weather machine," Papa Smurf said to Handy. "But it's just too dangerous to try and smurf rain and sunshine whenever we want it."

Handy was sad, but he knew what Papa Smurf said was true.

Poet Smurf was in the mood to write again. But now that the weather was sunny, he missed the rain.

I love the rain! I'm going to smurf a poem about the rain! he thought.

To get inspired, Poet Smurf wanted a spring shower. But he decided he didn't need a fancy weather machine – a little watering can worked just fine!